Goldilocks
and
the Three Bears

Illustrated by

Mike and Carl Gordon

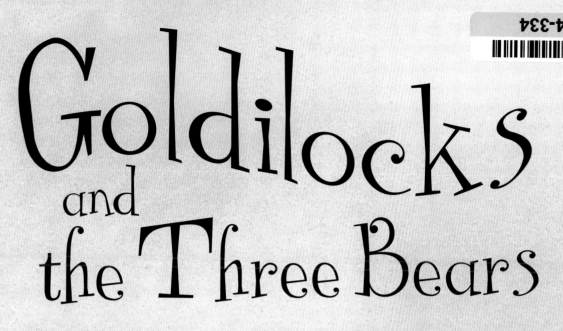

Retold by Susanna Davidson

Once upon a time, there was a little girl called...

GOLDILOCKS!

She liked to do something naughty each day.

MONDAY...

TUESDAY...

WEDNESDAY...   Goldi

THURSDAY...

"Now..." thought Goldilocks. "What shall I do next?"

Goldilocks' mother always said, "Don't go into the forest. It's full of big, scary bears."

But Goldilocks wasn't scared.
So on Friday, she went into the forest.

...a pretty little cottage.

"I wonder who lives here?" thought Goldilocks, and went inside.

"Mmm..." she said.
On the table were three
delicious-smelling bowls of porridge.

"I'm sure no one would mind if I had a tiny taste,"
thought Goldilocks.

First, Goldilocks tried the great, big bowl.

Next, she tried the middle-sized bowl.

OW!
Too hot!

Last of all, Goldilocks
tried the tiny bowl.

"Yum! Yum!" she said.
"Just right!"

And she ate it ALL up.

Feeling full, Goldilocks
looked for somewhere to sit.

First, she tried
the great, big chair.

Next, she tried the
middle-sized chair.

Last of all,
she tried the tiny chair.

"Aha!" thought Goldilocks.
"Just right." Until...

CRACK!

The chair broke.

"Oops!" said Goldilocks. "Time for a nap."

Upstairs, she found a great, big bed.

Too hard!

Next, she tried the middle-sized bed.

Too soft!

Last of all, she tried the tiny bed.
"Just right," said Goldilocks,
snuggling down.

Snore! Snore! Snore!

As she slept, a large paw pulled open the front door.

Three bears plodded into the house.

There was...

a great big father bear,

a middle-sized mother bear

and a tiny little baby bear.

"Who's been eating *my* porridge?"
growled Father Bear.

"Who's been eating *my* porridge?" gasped Mother Bear.

"Who's been eating *my* porridge?" squeaked Baby Bear.

They've eaten it all up!

Father Bear looked
around the room.

"Who's been sitting in
my chair?" he growled.

"Well! Who's been
sitting in *my* chair?"
howled Mother Bear.

"Who's been sitting in *my* chair?"
squeaked Baby Bear.

"They've broken it!"

They
heard
a rumbling
("snore")
coming
from
the
bedroom.

The three bears
climbed the
stairs.

"Who's been sleeping in *my* bed?" growled Father Bear.

"Who's been sleeping in *my* bed?"
wailed Mother Bear.

"Who's been sleeping in *my* bed?"
squeaked Baby Bear.

"She's still there!"

Goldilocks woke up and
SCREAMED!

She flew out of the cottage and ran all the way home, crying...

"I'll NEVER, EVER be naughty again."

Nor did Goldilocks EVER go into the forest again.

Edited by Jenny Tyler and Lesley Sims
Designed by Caroline Spatz
Cover design by Louise Flutter